ISBN 0 86163 077 7

© Award Publications Limited 1983

Spring House, Spring Place

London N.W. 5

Printed in Belgium

PUSS IN BOOTS

Illustrated by RENE CLOKE

AWARD PUBLICATIONS — LONDON

PUSS IN BOOTS

Jan, Hans and Robin were the sons of a miller.

When the miller died, he left his mill to Jan, his donkey to Hans and to his youngest son, Robin, he left his cat.

Puss was a very fine cat but, when Robin saw his brothers going off to work at the mill, he wondered what *he* should do for a living.

"I'm very fond of you, Puss," he said, "but I can't even buy you fish and milk."

"Don't worry," answered Puss, twirling his long whiskers, "I'm clever enough for both of us; just do as I suggest and all will be well.

First of all, make me a pair of strong boots and give me a hat and a sack."

Robin didn't know what Puss was planning, but as he hadn't any ideas of his own, he set to work and made a little pair of boots and found a hat and an empty sack for his cat.

"These will do very well," said Puss, "and the boots are excellent."

He put them on, threw the sack over his shoulder and, setting his hat jauntily on his head, he waved good-bye to Robin.

Robin watched him walk up the lane towards the common, the little boots going pit-a-pat and the wind blowing the feather in the cat's hat.

When Puss reached
the common, he put
the sack on the grass
and propped it open with a stick. Then he put
some parsley in the sack and tied a long string
to the stick.

Taking the end of the string in his paw,
Puss crept behind a bush and waited.

5

After a little while, three plump rabbits came out of their burrow and looked at the sack.

"That smells like parsley," said one.

"And it looks like parsley," said the second.

"Let's find out," suggested the third.

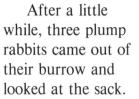

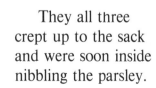

They all three crept up to the sack and were soon inside nibbling the parsley.

"Now's my chance," murmured Puss and he gave the string a sharp pull.

This closed the sack with the rabbits inside and Puss sprang from the bush and flung the sack over his shoulder.

Puss now set off for the King's palace and demanded to see His Majesty.

The footman at the door looked rather surprised at the strange caller but he took Puss along many corridors and into the King's room.

Puss gave a graceful bow.

"I have brought you a present of some rabbits from my master, the Marquis of Carabas, Your Majesty," he said.

"That is very kind," replied the King; "give my compliments to your master and here is a gold coin for yourself."

Puss bought himself a fine coat and hurried back to his master.

The next trick the clever cat played was to set his trap in a wood and scatter grain in it.

Very soon, two pigeons came along and started eating the grain.

Quick as lightning, Puss pulled the string and caught the birds.

These he took to the King with another kind message from the Marquis of Carabas.

A little while after this, Puss heard the news that the King and his daughter were going to drive by the river the next day.

"Now listen to my advice," said Puss to Robin. "Make your way to the river tomorrow for a swim and good fortune will come your way."

Robin followed Puss's advice but while he was bathing, Puss took his clothes and hid them behind a bush.

11

Before long, the King's coach came by and Puss sprang into the road.

"Stop! Stop!" he cried, "the Marquis of Carabas has had his clothes stolen while he was bathing in the river!"

The King was distressed to hear this and at once sent one of his servants to fetch a grand suit from the palace.

When Robin was
dressed he looked
very handsome and
thanked the King
for his kindness.

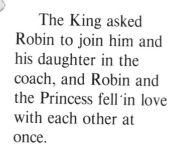

The King asked
Robin to join him and
his daughter in the
coach, and Robin and
the Princess fell in love
with each other at
once.

Puss ran ahead of the coach and called out to some men who were cutting corn,

"You must tell the King that these fields of corn belong to the Marquis of Carabas or he will have you all chopped into pieces!"

The men were so terrified that, when the King came driving by, they assured him that the fields belonged to the Marquis of Carabas.

Puss now ran past a fine farm and called out to the farmer,

"Tell the King that the land and all these animals belong to the Marquis of Carabas or you will be chopped into little bits!"

"Oh, yes, most certainly," answered the farmer in great alarm, "I will do as you say."

The King was very impressed when he heard this and decided that the Marquis of Carabas must be a very rich man.

16

Puss was well ahead of the King's coach and he now came to a castle where a very fierce Ogre lived.

Most people would have been frightened but not Puss.

"Is it true that you can change yourself into anything you like?"

"It certainly is true," boasted the Ogre.

"It sounds impossible," said Puss; "please show me how it is done."

In a moment the Ogre turned himself into a lion.

This *did* alarm Puss.

He sprang out of the window and continued the conversation from the roof until the Ogre had become his right shape again.

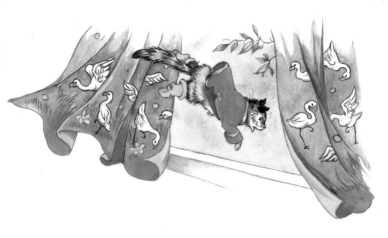

"That was certainly very clever," said
Puss, "but I suppose it would be more
difficult to turn yourself into something
small — perhaps a rat or a mouse? That I
expect you would find impossible."

The Ogre growled at Puss; he was very
vain and very stupid and no match for the
clever Puss.

"Nothing easier!"
he boasted, "just
watch me!"

In a flash, the fierce Ogre became a mouse.

"Ha! Ha!" laughed Puss; "now is my chance," and with a nimble spring he caught the mouse and killed it.

"Brains will win every time," he murmured.

Puss had now nearly finished his plans.

He ran through the castle, telling all the servants that the Ogre was dead and that the castle now belonged to the Marquis of Carabas.

"Hurray!" cried all the maids and men, "the Ogre was a cruel master and we shall be glad to have a new one."

"Prepare food for a grand feast," Puss told them, "for the King is coming to dine at the castle."

Puss was waiting at the gate to greet the King, the Princess and Robin.

"Welcome to the castle of the Marquis of Carabas!" he cried and led them to the dining hall.

23

Robin felt rather bewildered by all the
strange happenings of that day but he
was quite ready to become the Marquis
of Carabas and leave all the planning to
clever Puss.

A fine Banquet was soon ready, for
the servants were delighted to serve their
new master.

A little later, there was another happy occasion and another grand feast, for Robin married the Princess and there was great joy in the castle.

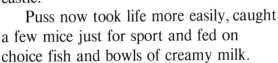

Puss now took life more easily, caught a few mice just for sport and fed on choice fish and bowls of creamy milk.